SCIENCE FICTIONISMS

SCIENCE FICTIONISMS

Compiled by William Rotsler

Salt Lake City

This is a Peregrine Smith Book, published by
Gibbs Smith, Publisher
P.O. Box 667
Layton, Utah 84041

Design by Scott Van Kampen
Editor: Gail Yngve
Front cover art by Bob Eggleton

Printed and bound in the United States

ISBN 0-87905-693-2 (pbk.)

CONTENTS

....

The only

"ism" that has

justified itself is

"pessimism."

George Orwell

WITT

This universe never did make sense; I suspect it was built on a government contract.

Robert A. Heinlein

❋

Would a precognitive telepath know what you were thinking before you thought it?

Sherry M. Gottlieb

CISMS

Every passing hour brings the solar system forty-three thousand miles closer to the Globular Cluster M13 in Hercules—and still there are some misfits who insist that there is no such thing as progress.

Kurt Vonnegut, Jr.

✳

Ugliness is nature's

contraceptive.

Gregory Benford

I belong to a hungry family—my mother used to count us after every meal.

Bob Shaw

Pray before meals—especially if your wife is a bad cook.

Kathleen Sky

The best measure of a man's honesty isn't his income tax return. It's the zero adjustment on his bathroom scale.

Arthur C. Clarke

Say what you will, lightning is one hellava murder weapon. The only problem, of course, is aiming it.

David Gerrold

It was no wonder that people were so horrible when they started life as children.

Kingsley Amis

✳

SCIENCE FICTIONISMS

(On retirement savings)
Gone today,
here tomorrow.

*Catherine Crook
de Camp*

＊

Anybody who'd kill my
wife for what I could
afford to pay is too stupid
to avoid arrest.

Alexis A. Gilliland

Power ennobles.
Absolute power
ennobles absolutely.

Harlan Ellison

Dying is putting all
your aches in one
casket.

Forrest J. Ackerman

Overachievement is giving yourself a
high colonic with a Roto-Rooter.

Robert Bloch

✳

SCIENCE FICTIONISMS

If all the world's a stage and all the people merely players, who in bloody hell hired the director?

Charles L. Grant

Yield to temptation; it may not pass your way again.

Robert A. Heinlein

It's a good thing money can't buy happiness. We couldn't stand the commercials.

David Gerrold

✳

If men knew how often women looked at their rear ends, they would never wear their wallets in their back pockets.

Sherry M. Gottlieb

Sure I'm prejudiced! None of my best friends are idiots!

Larry Niven

✳

Adolescence is that
time of life when you
discover your ability to
be depressed.

David Gerrold

The best wedding vows
would be, "I, George,
promise you, Lola, to take
you seriously."

George Clayton Johnson

Love ain't nothing but
sex misspelled.

Harlan Ellison

Don't try too hard.
You might succeed.

Robert A. Heinlein

The family that stays
together may be
convicted of incest.

Robert Bloch

SCIENCE FICTIONISMS

Sturgeon's First Law:

Nothing is Absolutely so.

Sturgeon's Second Law:

Ninety percent of everything is crud.

Sturgeon's Third Law:

It is not possible to assemble a device
containing small parts without dropping one
of those parts in a deep-pile carpet.

✳ *Theodore Sturgeon*

The difference between the USA and the USSR is that the USSR hides their unemployed on collective farms, and the USA hides them in the Postal Service.

Alexis A. Gilliland, 1978

The meek shall inherit the earth; now let's check out who gets heaven.

J. Neil Shulman

One fact can change your whole point of view. For instance, did you know that King Kong was a lesbian? ✳

David Gerrold

Being right means never
having to say you're sorry.

Vernor Vinge

I could carve a better
man out of a banana.

Kurt Vonnegut, Jr.

The optimist believes
we live in the best of all
possible worlds. The
pessimist fears this
is true.

James Brach Cabell

For every inch of height
over 5'5", one loses ten
points of IQ.

Marta Randall, 5'2"

I figure everything
after three scotches
is philosophical.

Robert Bloch

Money is truthful. If a
man speaks of his honor,
make him pay cash.

Robert A. Heinlein

SCIENCE FICTIONISMS

A day without sunshine
is like . . . night.

Harlan Ellison

New York:
Skyscraper National Park

Kurt Vonnegut, Jr.

Adversity is why you
never made it; luck is
✳ why he did.

Jerry Sohl

A civilization is only as
good as its cooking.

Kathleen Sky

I haven't submitted
to psychoanalysis. I've
just decided to dread
one day at a time.

Isaac Asimov

Psychology has been
no more than a body of
observations in search
of a science.

Keith Laumer

The Three Laws of Infernal Dynamics:

1. An object in motion will always be headed in the wrong direction.

2. An object at rest will always be in the wrong place.

3. The energy necessary to change either of these states is always more than you wish to expend, but never so much as to be totally impractical.

David Gerrold

✳

Money is a powerful
aphrodisiac. But flowers
work almost as well.

Robert A. Heinlein

Never let your sense of
morals prevent you from
doing what is right!

Isaac Asimov

✳

SCIENCE FICTIONISMS

The reason men are
greater than animals isn't
because we can dream
of the stars . . . it's
because we have some-
thing they haven't. Greed.

Harlan Ellison

Time doesn't hurry for
any man, either.

✳ *Alexis A. Gilliland*

Those who abhor
history are compelled
to rewrite it.

David Gerrold

If a thing is not worth
doing, it is not worth
doing well.

Jerry Pournelle

With my kind of luck,
if I went blind, they'd give   ✳
me a seeing-eye dog
with cataracts.

Robert Bloch

Marta's First Law of the Universe:

Crap accumulates in geometric proportion to crap cleared away.

Marta's Second Law of the Universe:

The more things an item is designed to do, the less likely it is to do any of them very well.

Marta Randall

Listening is not the
same as talking.

Isaac Asimov

The only winner of
the War of 1812 was
Tchaikovsky.

David Gerrold

He who frights and
runs away lives to run
away another day.

Bob Shaw

SCIENCE FICTIONISMS

Delusions are often functional. A mother's opinions about her children's beauty, intelligence, goodness, etcetera ad nauseum, keep her from drowning them at birth.

Robert A. Heinlein

Life ain't easy. But then, if it was, everybody would be doing it.

Harlan Ellison

Paperwork is the invention of the devil.

Alexis A. Gilliland

I don't shoot a man for being incompetent in the devil's work. I shoot him for being competent in the devil's work. Admiration for his technique is part of the process.

Larry Niven

Los Angeles goes on and on long after it has made its point.

Gregory Benford

Life is a simile.

Terry Carr

SCIENCE FICTIONISMS

There are two corrolaries to Murphy's Law ("If anything can go wrong, it will.") 1. It already has; they just haven't told you. 2. They lie a lot.

Elizabeth A. Lynn

Some people have one-track gutters.

Harlan Ellison

✳

An anthropologist should never make premises he can't keep.

Spider Robinson

Get a shot off fast. This
upsets him long enough
to let you get your
second shot perfect.

Robert A. Heinlein

It's better to be a live
coward than a dead
coward.

Robert Bloch

*

When you pass the buck,

don't ask for change.

David Gerrold

A fool: anyone who

thinks he sees what God

is doing.

Kurt Vonnegut, Jr.

I want revenge. I'll

accept justice. Mercy is

negotiable, but not very.

Alexis A. Gilliland

There are only two things
in the universe that vio-
late the law of conserva-
tion of energy: one is the
Road Runner, the other is
the Coyote. You can't do
it, and neither can I.

Diane Duane

Credit is the only endur-
ing testimonial to man's
confidence in man.

James Blish

Isn't it amazing how much fun two people can have just by taking off their clothes?

David Gerrold

The only completely consistent people are dead.

Aldous Huxley

There is no reason why good can't triumph as often as evil. The triumph of anything is a matter of organization. If there are such things as angels, I hope that they are organized along the lines of the Mafia.

Kurt Vonnegut, Jr.

Being intelligent is not a felony. But most societies evaluate it as being at least a misdemeanor.

Robert A. Heinlein

Malpractice makes malperfect.

David Gerrold

The trouble with hell is that the ambient temperature is above the flash point of alcohol. Which means you can't linger over your drink.

Alexis A. Gilliland

＊

The only defense against the weapons of the future is to prevent them from ever being used.

Arthur C. Clarke

The future is always going to be a lot like the present. People don't change as fast as their toys.

Sterling Blake (Gregory Benford)

✳ **FUTUR**

If you want a picture of the future, imagine a boot stamping on the human face—forever . . . and remember that it is forever.

George Orwell

S M S

*

SCIENCE FICTIONISMS

This is the first age
that's paid much atten-
tion to the future, which
is ironic since we may
not have one.

Arthur C. Clarke

It's a pity that taxpayers
don't read science
fiction. They might know
about the age they're
buying.

Frederik Pohl

The future is up for grabs. It belongs to any and all who will take the risk and accept the responsibility of consciously creating the future they want.

Robert Anton Wilson

The concept of progress acts as a protective mechanism to shield us from the terrors of the future.

Frank Herbert

✳

Your children will see the stars.

Robert A. Heinlein

SCIENCE FICTIONISMS

The future isn't what it
used to be.

Arthur C. Clarke

Future history will be a
race between education
and catastrophe.

H. G. Wells

The future arises out
of what goes on in the
present.

Norman Spinrad

✳

While I applaud attempts to think rigorously about the far future, it cannot be done by the simple extension of handy rules of thumbs. Other species, particularly, have other thumbs.

Gregory Benford

I am an optimist; anyone interested in the future has to be; otherwise, he would simply shoot himself.

Arthur C. Clarke

Science fiction is the anthropology of the future.

Joan Vinge

SCIENCE FICTIONISMS

In our field [science fiction], those who forget the past are unable to repeat it as the future.

Kathleen Sky

[Science fiction] is a concerned art form, for even in its shallowest version, it deals with tomorrow and the potentialities of man's place in it. . . . I write it because it refuses not to be written.

Harlan Ellison

✳

Robots make very
good friends because
they have very little
idea of what their own
self interest is.

Alexis A. Gilliland

You cannot go back
into the future.

Frank Herbert

A hundred years from
now, optical and radio
astronomers will find it
hard to believe that
serious observing was
ever possible on earth.

Arthur C. Clarke

*

POLIT

As long as men
worship the Caesars
and Napoleans, Caesars
and Napoleans will duly
rise and make them
miserable.

Aldous Huxley

CISMS

Men who think in life-times are of no use to statesmanship.

H. G. Wells

It is impossible for anyone to be responsible for another person's behavior. The most you or any leader can do is to encourage each one to be responsible for himself.

Robert A. Heinlein

Comedians and politicians each tell the audience what it wants to hear. The difference is that the audience laughs at the comedian and the politician laughs at the the audience.

Alexis A. Gilliland

The liberal of the species is always more dangerous because he always seems so much more rational.

David Gerrold

Don't assume merely because someone is the head of state of a country, he is also sane.

George Scithers

Autocracy is based on the assumption that one man is wiser than a million men. Let's play that over again, too. Who decides?

Robert A. Heinlein

Revolution's the easy part. Ruling afterwards—that's something else entirely.

Jerry Pournelle

✳

SCIENCE FICTIONISMS

Well, sure, the government lies, and newspapers lie, but in a democracy they aren't the same lies.

Alexis A. Gilliland

Power-hungry people, whom luck or personal faults have relegated to impotence, become revolutionaries. They hope that inversion of the social pyramid will automatically move them from bottom to top.

L. Sprague de Camp

✳

The idea that a government can give the people their freedom is ridiculous. Any power strong enough to give the people what they want is also powerful enough to take it away. Freedom is handmade. It only occurs when indviduals manufacture it for themselves.

David Gerrold

In a mature society, "civil servant" is semantically equal to "civil master."

Robert A. Heinlein

Tyranny goes with poverty; it's cheaper than democracy.

Larry Niven

✳

Idealism is the noble toga that political gentlemen drape over their will to power.

Aldous Huxley

The right to criticise the American government is strictly an American right—and it is the right that Americans will most vigorously defend against outsiders. Only an Amercian can say terrible things about the American government and mean it as wholeheartedly as he does.

David Gerrold

Now is the time for all good parties to come to the aid of man.

Karen Anderson

All animals are equal, but some animals are more equal than others.

George Orwell

Never accept the initial premise of the opposition.

John W. Campbell

✳

SCIENCE FICTIONISMS

When a politician says "order of magnitude," he means twenty to thirty percent. When he says "infinitely," he means two or three times. His closest approach to mathematical virtue is when he calls for a recount.

Alexis A. Gilliland

Our government has great confidence in its citizens—which is why it continues to overspend.

William Rotsler

A politician's success is measured by his ability to get elected. If he's good at that, he doesn't have to be good at much of anything else.

David Gerrold

Politics is just a name for the way we get things done . . . without fighting.

Robert A. Heinlein

Law-and-order candidates are rarely dangerous to criminals.

David Gerrold

There are no circumstances under which a state is justified in placing its welfare ahead of mine.

Robert A. Heinlein

✳

Most ignorance is vincible ignorance. We don't know because we don't want to know.

Aldous Huxley

Learning isn't a means to an end; it is an end in itself.

Robert A. Heinlein

EDUCAT

There are no things man
was not meant to know.
There are, perhaps, some
things man is too dumb
to figure out, but that's a
different problem.

Michael Kurland

ONISMS *

SCIENCE FICTIONISMS

A stupid man cannot learn, an ignorant man has not had the opportunity to learn, but a foolish man is able to learn, has the opportunity, and does not do it.

Chelsea Quinn Yarbro

If a man cannot explain in terms that any reasonably well-educated person can understand what he is talking about, there is an excellent chance that he himself does not know.

L. Sprague de Camp

I am not familiar with
what I want to know.

F. M. Busby

The problem with knowing
a little bit about everything
is remembering that it is
a little bit.

Kathleen Sky

It isn't knowledge that's   ✳
making trouble, but the
uses it's being put to.

Kurt Vonnegut, Jr.

History is filled with the sound of great minds meeting—head on.

Poul Anderson

The hardest lesson to learn is that learning is a continual process.

David Gerrold

A master's degree is the union card of the academic world.

Gregory Benford, Ph.D.

You can't trust self-education; it goes too far, gets too bloated, knows no moderation. If you know an instructor, then you only know the instructor. If you know the subject, you know the subject.

Roger Zelazny

Highly organized
research is guaranteed
to produce nothing new.

Frank Herbert

There is never much difficulty in obtaining information. Accuracy is another matter. And it's almost impossible to be sure your information is exclusive.

Robert Sheckley

A diploma only proves that you know how to look up an answer.

David Gerrold

Dullard: Someone who looks up a thing in the encyclopedia, turns directly to the entry, reads it, and then closes the book.

Philip José Farmer

✳

A man's knowledge is like an expanding sphere, the surface corresponding to the boundary between the known and the unknown. As the sphere grows, so does its surface; the more a man learns, the more he realizes how much he does not know. Hence, the most ignorant man thinks he knows it all.

L. Sprague de Camp

SCIENCE FICTIONISMS

A process cannot be understood by stopping it.
Understanding must move with the flow of the process,
must join it, and flow with it.

Frank Herbert

Experience teaches.
Novelty distracts.

David Gerrold

You learn by pleasure,
and you learn by pain.

Roger Zelazny

A little ignorance can
go a long way.

David Gerrold

You live and you learn,
or you don't live long.

Robert A. Heinlein

But need alone is not
enough to set power
free—there must be
knowledge.

Ursula K. Le Guin

Why do most people think that their own impoverished lives must be the norm of the universe?

Poul Anderson

If everything you know is wrong, then so are the scary parts, so relax.

Spider Robinson

*

Warning to time travelers: To assume that the taboos of your native culture are "natural" and that you can't go too wrong by behaving by the rules your loving parents taught you is to risk death. Or worse. If you think death has no "worse," read history.

Robert A. Heinlein

ISMS *

SCIENCE FICTIONISMS

The worst thing that could happen to anybody would be not to be used for anything by anybody.

Kurt Vonnegut, Jr.

Never be embarrassed by the things you cannot do. Be embarrassed by the things you can do and don't do well.

Len Wein

Life is routine punctuated by orgies.

Aldous Huxley

In a healthy society, dissent is free and can be endured. If you think that a sex-ridden society, or a permissive society, or a think-as-you-please society is not healthy, you have but to try the kind of society in which unbridled repression sees to it that you think, write, say, and do only what some dominating force says you may, and you will find out what an unhealthy society really is.

Isaac Asimov

✳

Nobody is ever ready
for anything. If they were
ready for it, there would
be no point in living
through it.

David Gerrold

Nothing gives you
more zest than running
for your life.

Robert A. Heinlein

Life is a bowl of cherries,
but the problem is—you
have to eat the pits, too.

David Bischoff

✳

We cannot foretell what will come of [life]. We do not know where we are going. Nor do most of us care. For us it is enough that we are on our way.

Poul Anderson

The joy of living, its beauty, is all bound up in the fact that life can surprise you.

Frank Herbert

*

It has been said that life is only a short biological process taking place on a very minor planet; but it's my process and my planet, and that makes it important to me.

Kathleen Sky

Learn the true topography: the monstrous and wonderful archetypes are not inside you, not inside your consciousness; you are inside them, trapped and howling to get out.

R. A. Lafferty

Fear is the feeling you get when you are in danger, the feeling that arises when you are unsure of your own capability to meet the situation.

Keith Laumer

Of course life is bizarre. The more bizarre it gets, the more interesting it is. The only way to approach it is to make yourself some popcorn and enjoy the show.

David Gerrold

✳

When action grows unprofitable, gather information; when information grows unprofitable, sleep.

Ursula K. Le Guin

Contentment is the continuing act of accepting the process of your own life.

David Gerrold

Once you remove the absurdity from human existence, there isn't much left.

Alexis A. Gilliland

Spare me from living
with worthy souls whose
bow of enthusiasm is
never allowed to rest
unstrung.

Edgar Pangborn

Certainly the game is
rigged. Don't let that
stop you; you don't
bet, you can't win.

Robert A. Heinlein

SCIENCE FICTIONISMS

Birth and death are the only two events in your life that you can be positive will happen to you.

Kathleen Sky

Don't look now, but you're on the firing line in the big revolution.

Harlan Ellison

*

It may be that the kind of life that exists on the earth is only one small subset of a vast array of possible biologies.

Carl Sagan

Laughing or crying is what a human being does when there's nothing else he can do.

Kurt Vonnegut, Jr.

Boredom sets in when you have nothing to occupy your mind or when instinct says, "The activity at hand is not vital to my survival."

Keith Laumer

Pessimist by policy, optimist by temperament—it is possible to be both. How? By never taking an unnecessary chance and by minimizing risks you can't afford. This permits you to play out the game happily, untroubled by the certainty of the outcome.

Robert A. Heinlein

The secret of the universe is this: the universe doesn't care. That part of the job is yours.

David Gerrold

Never count a human
dead until you've seen
the body. And even then
you can make a mistake.

Frank Herbert

There would be little
sense to existence did
boys have no chance to
be more than their
fathers.

Poul Anderson

We are what we pretend
to be, so we must be
careful about what we
pretend to be.

Kurt Vonnegut, Jr.

*

Literature thrives on taboos, just as all art thrives on technical difficulties.

Anthony Burgess

Few artists thrive in solitude, and nothing is more stimulating than the conflict of minds with similar interests.

Arthur C. Clarke

A R T

True genius can be identified by the fact that its expression changes the world into something it has never been before.

David Gerrold

A culture is only as great as its dreams, and its dreams are dreamed by artists.

L. Ron Hubbard

ISMS *

SCIENCE FICTIONISMS

Don't think! Thinking is the enemy of creativity. It's self-conscious, and anything self-conscious is lousy. You can't try to do things. You simply must do things.

Ray Bradbury

Creative work, of however humble a kind, is the source of man's most solid, least transitory happiness.

Aldous Huxley

Literature is recognizable
through its capacity to
evoke more than it says.

Anthony Burgess

It is the function of the
artist to make arbitrary
choices.

John Shirley

All art is a fight against
decay.

Brian Aldiss

MILITA

Command must always look confident. All that faith riding on your shoulders while you sit in the critical seat and never show it.

Frank Herbert

RYISMS

Saying that the deterrent prevents nuclear war because we haven't had one yet is like saying that my leg is unbreakable because I've never broken it.

John Brunner

Niven's First Law: Never throw shit at an armed man. *Corollary:* Never stand next to someone who is throwing ✳ shit at an armed man.

Larry Niven

SCIENCE FICTIONISMS

Half an officer's
training is learning
what not to see.

Jerry Pournelle

It's better to look the
other way than to com-
mand ineffectually.

Walter M. Miller, Jr.

✳ Ideas and not battles
mark the forward
progress of mankind.

L. Ron Hubbard

He had grown up in a country run by politicians who sent the pilots to man the bombers to kill the babies to make the world safe for children to grow up in.

Ursula K. Le Guin

Grief is the price of victory.

Frank Herbert

We say we love peace, but it doesn't excite us. Even pacifists talk more about the horrors of war than about the glories of peace.

Jerry Pournelle

The Roman Empire did not fall because the Romans were decadent and had orgies. When they were the most decadent and threw the wildest orgies, they conquered the Mediterranean world. When they reformed and adopted Christianity, the barbarians conquered them.

L. Sprague de Camp

✳ Peace should not depend on force.

D. C. Fontana

Like changing the guard
at Buckingham Palace,
military customs die hard
and slowly.

Michael Kurland

So long as man's courage
endures, he will conquer;
upon the courage in his
heart all things depend.

H. G. Wells

The test of a society is
whether or not you, your
family, and friends can
live in it safely.

L. Ron Hubbard

Quantity produces quality. If you only write a few things, you're doomed.

Ray Bradbury

Read at least one book a day. Study the memoirs of authors who interest you.

Arthur C. Clarke

* WRITIN

I have been successful probably because I have always realized that I knew nothing about writing and have merely tried to tell an interesting story entertainingly.

Edgar Rice Burroughs

GISMS

*

The reader has certain rights. He bought your story. Think of this as an implicit contract. He's entitled to be entertained, instructed, amused; maybe all three. If he quits in the middle, or puts the book down feeling his time has been wasted, you're in violation.

Larry Niven

The unread story is not a story; it is little black marks on wood pulp. The reader reading it makes it live: a live thing, a story.

Ursula K. Le Guin

Individual science fiction stories may seem as trivial as ever to the blinder critics and philosophers of today—but the core of science fiction, its essence, has become crucial to our salvation if we are to be saved at all.

Isaac Asimov

[On banned books]: Run to the bookstore and get that book. If the school board tells you you can't read it, it's probably what you need.

Stephen King

✳

Short stories are designed to deliver their impact in as few pages as possible. A tremendous amount is left out, and a good short story writer learns to include only the most essential information.

Orson Scott Card

✳

James Blish told me I had the worst case of "said bookism" (that is, using every word except said to indicate dialogue). He told me to limit the verbs to said, replied, asked, and answered and only when absolutely necessary.

Anne McCaffrey

In writing a series of stories about the same characters, plan the whole series in advance in some detail to avoid contradictions and inconsistencies.

L. Sprague de Camp

Books aren't written; they're rewritten. Including your own. It is one of the hardest things to accept, especially after the seventh rewrite hasn't quite done it.

Michael Crichton

Resist the temptation to use dazzling style to conceal the weakness of substance.

Stanley Schmidt

SCIENCE FICTIONISMS

Everything is becoming science fiction. From the margins of an almost invisible literature has sprung the intact reality of the twentieth century.

J. G. Ballard

If science fiction is the mythology of modern technology, then its myth is tragic.

Ursula K. Le Guin

＊

There is no unemployment insurance for freelance writers.

Robert A. Heinlein

If I ever discover a definition of science fiction,
I shall immediately attempt to violate it.

Roger Zelazny

Science fiction is that branch of literature that deals
with human responses to changes in the level of
science and technology.

Isaac Asimov

The pen is noisier than
the sword.

Marta Randall

SCIENCE FICTIONISMS

If you can't annoy somebody, there's little point in writing.

Kingsley Amis

1. Find a subject you care about.
2. Do not ramble, though.
3. Keep it simple.
4. Have the guts to cut.
5. Sound like yourself.
6. Say what you mean to say.
7. Pity the readers.

Kurt Vonnegut, Jr.

✳

If you have other things in your life—family, friends, good, productive day work—these things can interact with your writing and the sum will be all the richer.

David Brin

Be anything you want to be, but don't be dull.

Frank Robinson

Writing for a penny a word is ridiculous. If a man wanted to make a million dollars, the best way would be to start his own religion.

L. Ron Hubbard

✳

The trouble with a lot of people who try to write is they intellectualize about it. That comes later. The intellect is given to us by God to test things once they're something, not to worry about things ahead of time.

Ray Bradbury

Thinking is the activity I like best, and writing is simply thinking through my fingers.

Isaac Asimov

We in the writing profession have this technical term for people who attribute the opinions of characters to the author himself; we call them "idiots."

Larry Niven

In the first person, anything can be made to sound credible.

George Orwell

Talent is extremely common. What is rare is the willingness to endure the life of a writer.

Kurt Vonnegut, Jr.

✳

In our field, those who
forget the past are
unable to repeat it as
the future.

Kathleen Sky

Science Fiction writers
do have their blind spots
despite the fact that
we're all geniuses, we're
all marvelous people, and
some of us can spell.

Isaac Asimov

Clarion 1978 Rules of Writing:

1. Use other words.

2. In a different order, too.

3. Make all the scenes more real.

4. Try using a plot.

5. Oh yeah—characters.

Terry Carr and others

There is nothing
more unreal than unreal
science fiction.

Norman Spinrad

SCIENCE FICTIONISMS

Three Rules for Literary Success:

1. Read a lot.

2. Write a lot.

3. Read a lot more, write a lot more.

Robert Silverberg

A reviewer tells you whether you'll probably enjoy a given book or not; a critic tells you why you shouldn't—or in rare cases—should have when you didn't.

Spider Robinson

The normal curve of a writer's income is steadily up.
But the point from which the curve starts is zero.

Frederik Pohl

Science fiction is no more written for scientists than ghost stories are written for ghosts.

Brian Aldiss

It is a cardinal sin to bore the reader.

Larry Niven

✳

If you're not trying to communicate, you sure don't belong in the writing game.

Ursula K. Le Guin

Discipline in writing equals professionalism.

Dorothy C. Fontana

A critic is a man who creates nothing and thereby feels qualified to judge the work of creative men. There is a logic in this; he is unbiased—he hates all creative people equally.

Robert A. Heinlein

If the approach to writing can be classified at all, I would be tempted to dichotomize: those who start as storytellers, and those who start as wordsmiths, poets. The drive of the story pushes the storyteller into clumsy phrases, purple prose, redundancies, but he has a story complete with beginning, middle and end. Things happen and there is resolution. The wordsmiths often have collages of beautifully sketched images and little else.

Kate Wilhelm

A writer is a perpetual notion machine.

David Gerrold

Heinlein's Rules:

1. You must write.

2. You must finish what you write.

3. You must refrain from rewriting except to editorial order.

4. You must put it on the market until sold.

Robert A. Heinlein

(Ellison's Additions)

5. Only accept the last four words of rule three if your integrity and the quality / logic of the story reconcile such changes. Otherwise:

6. Kill to retain the integrity of your work.

Harlan Ellison

I think the reason there are so few literary prodigies is that adolescents don't know enough about themselves or the world to depict human beings believably.

Darrell Schweitzer

You can't say, I won't write today, because that excuse will extend into several days, then several months, then . . . you are not a writer anymore, just someone who dreams about being a writer.

Dorothy C. Fontana

✳

109

SCIENCE FICTIONISMS

As a writer you are free. You are about the freest person that ever was. Your freedom is what you have bought with your solitude, your loneliness. You are in the country where you make up the rules, the laws. You are both dictator and obedient populace. It is a country nobody has ever explored before. It is up to you to make the maps, to build the cities. Nobody else in the world can do it, or ever could do it, or will ever be able to do it again.

Ursula K. Le Guin

*

Writing is the only job I know that your wife will nag you out of.

Frederik Pohl

Science fiction deals with improbable possibilities, fantasy with plausible impossibilities.

Miriam Allen deFord

God lets you write, but he also lets you not write.

Kurt Vonnegut, Jr.

Writing is not necessarily something to be ashamed of—but do it in private and wash your hands afterwards.

Robert A. Heinlein

ENVIRONN

Actually, all pollution is simply an unused resource. Garbage is the only raw material that we're too stupid to use.

Arthur C. Clarke

If Earth's children ever forget who provides for them, we may wake up someday and find we don't have a home.

Jean Auel

NTALISMS

The environment of any given place, at any given point in time, is the best it will ever be again.

Grania Davis

Disturbing the ecological balance is the worst mistake any government can make.

Robert A. Heinlein

＊

A moral choice in its basic terms appears to be a choice that favors survival, a choice made in favor of life.

Ursula K. Le Guin

You can't fool mother nature. (But she can fool you.)

G. Harry Stine

All of us understand the put and take of checking accounts, but few understand the careful accounts of deposits and withdrawals that nature keeps.

Albert Bester

The Earth is just too
small and fragile a basket
for the human race to
keep all its eggs in.

Robert A. Heinlein

The future has become uninhabitable. Such
hopelessness can arise, I think, only from an inability
to face the present, to live in the present, to live as a
responsible being among other beings in this sacred
world here and now, which is all we have and all
we need to found our hope upon.

Ursula K. Le Guin

PHYSIC

There are no absolute certainties in this universe.
A man must try to whip order into a yelping pack of
probabilities and uniform success is impossible.

Jack Vance

*

SISMS

As the record of the past shows, the most interesting and important events are usually those that were never predicted: history, like much of physics, is often discontinuous.

Arthur C. Clarke

Information can't be put in any container that isn't leaky.

Spider Robinson

✳

SCIENCE FICTIONISMS

There is no such thing as the supernatural; there are only things we don't understand yet.

Kathleen Sky

Color is to light what pitch is to sound.

Carl Sagan

Science is made up of many things that appear obvious after they are explained.

Frank Herbert

✳

Time is what keeps everything from happening at once.

Robert Bloch

Space is what stops everything from happening in the same place.

Arthur C. Clarke

Progress in physics is achieved by denying the obvious and accepting the impossible.

Robert A. Heinlein

✳

The most merciful
thing in the world is the
inability of the human
mind to correlate all
its contents.

H. P. Lovecraft

T R U

*

New and stirring things are belittled because if they are not belittled, the humiliating question arises: why then are you not taking part in them?

H. G. Wells

Thin people are thin because they don't know any better.

Isaac Asimov

ISMS *

SCIENCE FICTIONISMS

Losers don't forget
as fast as winners.

Gregory Benford

Being right too soon is
socially unacceptable.

Robert A. Heinlein

For every Gandhi or
Nader or Bertrand
Russell or Thoreau,
there are a hundred
thousand Nixons.

Harlan Ellison

You can't enslave a free man. The only person who can do that to a man is himself. The most you can do to a free man is to kill him.

Robert A. Heinlein

To be free, one must first want to be free; to want to be free, one must know what freedom is.

Chester Anderson

The universe did not invent justice. Man did. Unfortunately, man must reside in the universe.

Roger Zelazny

✳

SCIENCE FICTIONISMS

A leader is one thing that distinguishes a mob from a people. He maintains the level of individuals. Too few individuals and a people revert to a mob.

Frank Herbert

The opposite of love is not hate, but indifference.

Frank Robinson

There is such a thing as having too much liberty. Not so, you say? Just imagine if your neighbors had unlimited freedom.

William Rotsler

The final frontier is not space; it is the human soul. Space is merely the place in which that frontier will be met.

David Gerrold

Now is what's between where you've been and where you're going.

Sherry M. Gottlieb

I don't try to predict the future; I try to prevent it.

Ray Bradbury

✳

Lies are the mortar that binds the savage
individual man into the social masonry.

H. G. Wells

A little ignorance can go a long way.

David Gerrold

It has yet to be proven
that intelligence has
survival value.

Arthur C. Clarke

The most hopelessly stu-
pid man is he who is not
aware that he is wise.

Isaac Asimov

You can go wrong
by being too skeptical
as readily as by being
too trusting.

Robert A. Heinlein

A flung stone has always
been a fool's favorite
means of putting himself
on a level with the wise.

Edgar Pangborn

✳

Give Neanderthal man a shave and a haircut, dress him in well-fitting clothes, and he could probably walk down New York's Fifth Avenue without getting much notice.

Isaac Asimov

Hope clouds observations.

Frank Herbert

A person who speaks cleverly is witty; one who asks questions is smart.

Terry Carr

Whatever is funny is subversive; every joke is ultimately a custard pie. A dirty joke is a sort of mental revolution.

George Orwell

A person who *won't* be blackmailed *can't* be blackmailed.

Robert A. Heinlein

Improve a mechanical device and you may double productivity. But improve man, you gain a thousandfold.

Gene L. Coon and Carey Wilbur

✳

SCIENCE FICTIONISMS

Clarke's Laws:

1. When a distinguished but elderly scientist states that something is possible, he is almost certainly right. When he states that something is impossible, he is probably wrong.

2. The only way to discover the limits of the possible is to look beyond into the impossible.

3. Any sufficiently advanced technology is indistinguishable from magic.

Arthur C. Clarke

✳

Aphrodisiacs come in strange forms.

Terry Carr

Crude classifications
and false generalizations
are the curse of
organized human life.

H. G. Wells

It takes two to create a
heaven, but hell can be
accomplished by one.

Robert A. Heinlein

We are healthy only to
the extent that our ideas
are humane.

Kurt Vonnegut, Jr.

*

SCIENCE FICTIONISMS

"Cynical" is a term
invented by optimists to
describe realists.

Gregory Benford

The truth of a proposition
has nothing to do with its
credibility.

Robert A. Heinlein

*

The secret of a successful restaurant is sharp knives.

George Orwell

Justice, in the common meaning of the term, will never be attained without two measures. One is the substitution of computers for judges and juries. The other is a lie detector that really works.

L. Sprague de Camp

There is no merit in discipline under ideal circumstances. I'll have it in the face of death, or it's useless.

Isaac Asimov

The difference between love and infatuation is that love ties a knot in the end of the rope.

Alexis A. Gilliland

✳

133

SCIENCE FICTIONISMS

It pays to be obvious,
especially if you have a
reputation for subtlety.

Isaac Asimov

If a thing is worth doing,
it's worth doing for
money.

David Gerrold

✳ Thoughts, like fleas, jump
from man to man. But
they don't bite everybody.

Stanislaw Lem

There is probably no more terrible instant of enlightenment than the one in which you discover your father is a man—with human flesh.

Frank Herbert

The number of things a tool is designed to do varies inversely with how well it will do any one of them.

George Scithers

Scoundrels are predictable, but you're a man of honor, and that frightens me.

Robert A. Heinlein

✳

SCIENCE FICTIONISMS

A man receiving charity practically always hates his benefactor—it is a fixed characteristic of human nature.

George Orwell

If someone keeps having things go wrong, try out the assumption that it's because that someone wants them to go wrong.

George Scithers

✳

Civilization is the way one's own people live. Savagery is the way foreigners live.

Octavia Butler

Humans are almost

always lonely.

Frank Herbert

That which is never

attempted never

transpires.

Jack Vance

Even a mirror will not

show you yourself if you   *

do not wish to see.

Roger Zelazny

Dignity is not only knowing when to duck, it's also knowing how to look like a gourmet when you take a pie in the face.

Harlan Ellison

Facts do not cease to exist because they are ignored.

Aldous Huxley

There is no place in modern society for a man who is not a misfit.

Lee Hoffman

The only thing worse
than learning the truth is
not learning the truth.

David Gerrold

Formal courtesy between
a husband and a wife is
even more important than
it is between strangers.

Robert A. Heinlein

✳

Moral indignation is
jealousy with a halo.

H. G. Wells

Half of being smart is knowing what you're dumb at.

David Gerrold

*

I've always thought that the power of any country is the sum total of its individuals. Each individual is rich with ideas, with concepts, rich with his own revolution.

Ray Bradbury

Parting with people is a sadness; a place is only a place.

Frank Herbert

Hate comes from the
past, fear from the future.
Pain and pleasure are
now, and therefore
their own trap.

Steven Barnes

Everybody lies about sex.

Robert A. Heinlein

✳

What matters in history was not what men
thought but what they felt.

Poul Anderson

Be patient with your children when they are young so that they will be patient with you when you are old.

Kathleen Sky

A faith that cannot survive collision with the truth is not worth many regrets.

Arthur C. Clarke

The true function of the mass population is the production, by their sheer numbers, of the occasional genius.

Keith Laumer

A woman is not property, and husbands who think otherwise are living in a dream world.

Robert A. Heinlein

The trouble with getting in free is that you can't get your money back.

David McDaniel

Work is the only thing you do for years without getting the habit.

Bob Shaw

✳

Clarke's Law of Revolutionary Ideas:

Every revolutionary idea—in science, politics, art, or whatever—evokes three stages of reaction. They may be summed up by three phrases:

1. "It's crazy—don't waste my time."

2. "It's possible—but not worth doing."

3. "I said it was a good idea all along. . . ."

Arthur C. Clarke

*

Faith strikes me as intellectual laziness.

Robert A. Heinlein